CONTENTS

1	Invisible	1
2	The Griffin Map	12
3	Celia's Shop	22
4	Large and ... Scary	29
5	Into the Forest	36
6	The Den	41
7	Teleporting: Rule One	50
8	Midnight Footsteps	60
9	The Mayor's Plan	70
10	Wing Chop	79
11	The Truth	91
12	Wardens	99

1

Invisible

Rain dribbled down the windows of Griffin House and the skies were a dismal grey. The weather perfectly matched Grace Griffin's mood.

Grace sat on her bed, pretending not to hear her mum knocking on the door.

"You have to go," said Watson, the family raven. He was perched on Grace's bedpost.

"No one will notice if I'm not there," said Grace.

There was a soft whirr of turning cogs as Watson spread his mechanical wings and ruffled his feathers.

The door swung open.

"Grace, come on!" said her mum, Ann. "Why aren't you wearing your uniform? It's not every day we're invited to the Mayor's office."

But what was the point, Grace thought, when she still had two years to wait before she was allowed to take part in a real mission? "Do I have to go?" she asked. "I could stay and watch the map today."

"No," Mum replied. "And hurry up. Bren's waiting." Mum went to Grace's wardrobe and took her training uniform from the hanger. "Griffins stick together, Grace," Mum went on. "We have an important job and—"

"—Moreland relies on us wardens to keep the country safe," Grace finished. "I know." She took her uniform and began to get changed. It was a light brown jumpsuit with a gold symbol of a gate on the chest. There were pockets everywhere: the arms, the waist, the hips and the thighs. But Grace's favourite pocket was at the bottom of the leg, where the stun stick would be kept when she was finally allowed one. Each pocket contained an item of warden's equipment: notepad, rope, medi-kit and a variety of small tools. All lightweight for easy travel.

"Watson, will you watch the map while we're out?" Mum asked.

The Griffin map was the most important piece of technology in the city of Copperport. It showed the entire country of Moreland and included portals that let the Griffins travel into the map to help people. The Griffin family had been wardens of the map ever since Great Grandma Griffin had invented it. They helped to keep law and order in Moreland. Mum was a warden, and Grace's brother Bren too – now he was fifteen. Crime in the country had been halved since the invention of the map. Ann Griffin took the family's position as wardens very seriously.

"I would be delighted to watch the map," Watson said.

Grace huffed to herself.

"Grace, you're going, and that's that," Mum told her.

Grace, Ann and Bren walked along the wet streets of Copperport, rain pounding on their umbrellas and the many layered rooftops of the city. The hydro-mill, which supplied the city with power, turned slowly in the distance. It kicked up a strong, salty aroma from its position where the river met the sea.

Grace glanced at Bren. "You're walking like a peacock," she whispered. "And why is your hair all smoothed back like that?"

Bren scowled and pulled up the collar of his uniform.

Grace and Bren used to do everything together. But now that Bren could go out on missions, he was acting superior to Grace and wasn't interested in training with her. She sighed to herself. She was just as good as Bren at self-defence. Last week Grace had scored more points than him in the rescue simulator where they practised missions. Bren had accused Watson of helping her.

As they walked, everyone they passed greeted Ann Griffin with a nod or a word of thanks for keeping Moreland safe. Ann always smiled humbly and said it was an honour to be looking out for those in need.

Soon Grace, Bren and their mum were outside Mayor Pick's house. It was a tall red-brick building with a pillared entrance, the most impressive in the street. One of Mayor Pick's assistants led them up the stairs to a grand office. The golden-haired Mayor Pick sat behind a large desk, smiling in his green velvet jacket and ruffled-neck shirt.

"Ann, Bren, how lovely to see you!" Mayor Pick declared. "Do come in and sit down."

Grace looked down at herself, wondering if she'd become invisible.

Bren and Ann sat in the two seats in front of Mayor Pick's desk, which was covered in toppling piles of paper. Mayor Pick moved a stack to the side so that he could see Ann better. "It seems I spend my days signing pieces of paper," he said, smiling sadly with a small shrug.

Grace stood behind Ann and Bren, feeling like an unwanted guest at a party.

Mayor Pick turned to Bren and said, "Congratulations on your recent mission into the map! The way you handled the attempted bank robbery in Redwick really was incredible. The residents of Redwick have declared you a hero for putting a dangerous thief out of action with the swift use of a stun stick. Apparently the thief was planning a series of burglaries across towns in the east, which have now been prevented. It just shows how important the map is in keeping our country lawful."

Grace's eyes began to wander around the room as Mayor Pick continued to lavish more praise on Bren. She took in the oak shelves filled with books and many spyglasses.

Grace counted thirty-two spyglasses. *The Mayor must collect them*, she thought.

Bren began recounting the details of the mission and Grace shuffled quietly towards the shelves.

Her attention was caught by a large beautiful spyglass. It was crafted in rosewood and overlaid with a wave pattern and the Mayor's family crest, both in gold. The crest was a shield with a "P" in the centre and a galleon ship on the top. Grace took the spyglass from its holder and raised it to her eye.

"What are you doing?" Mayor Pick snapped.

Grace jumped and the spyglass slipped from her hands. She fumbled to catch it, but it clattered to the floor. Her back tensed.

Mum rushed over. "Grace!" she said with quiet force.

"Sorry," Grace said, and flashed an apologetic smile at Mayor Pick.

Mum picked up the spyglass and replaced it on the shelf. "I'm very sorry, Mayor Pick," Mum said. "Do forgive my daughter. She's keen but gets easily distracted."

Bren rolled his eyes while Grace followed Mum back to the desk and stood behind the chairs.

"As I was saying," the Mayor continued, "I would like to give you one of my spyglasses as a reward, Bren. I don't give them to just anyone, you know." The Mayor glanced at Grace and frowned.

"They're very precious," Mum said. "We can't possibly accept, Mayor Pick."

Bren slumped in his chair.

"Nonsense, Ann," the Mayor argued. "And call me Clemence. After all, we did go to Copperport Academy of Science together."

Mum smiled, but Grace knew she would keep calling him Mayor Pick because Mum did everything *by the rules*. Like not allowing Grace to go on a mission until she was fifteen, no matter how much Grace begged.

The Mayor put a spyglass on his desk in front of Bren. It was just like the one Grace had picked up.

"It's beautiful," said Bren.

"My family have crafted spyglasses for generations," said Mayor Pick. "We've become rather good at them!"

Bren accepted the spyglass and another of the Mayor's assistants saw them to the door.

Outside, Mum and Bren both turned to Grace.

"Can't you stop fidgeting for one moment?" Bren snapped. "I was so embarrassed when you dropped that spyglass!" He stormed off ahead.

Mum shook her head. "Your time will come, Grace," she said.

2

The Griffin Map

A few days later, Grace and Bren were in the Griffin map room. Grace was repairing a broken stun stick while Bren was polishing his spyglass, which now took pride of place on the mantelpiece.

The map room was the heart of their home. The high walls were lined with shelves heavy with books and mission tools, and a large painting of Great Grandma Griffin hung above the mantelpiece. The room was painted the blue of a clear evening sky, with golden stars dotted all around. A brassy globe with orbiting moons

hung from the centre of the high ceiling, and
beneath it was the most important thing of all.

The Griffin map.

The map was laid out on a huge table. It was made of thick paper and showed all the towns and villages of Moreland. It had been created so that even the most remote places could call for help. Each town or village had its own electrical Griffin gate on the map. These ornate golden gates looked like the sort that formed the entrance to a grand country home.

When a call came in from a town or village that needed help, their gate flashed a different colour. If the gate flashed red, it was an emergency. Blue was for small incidents, like a cat stuck up a tree, a lost item or a minor argument between townsfolk. (Mum sometimes moaned that people these days were unwilling to think for themselves and called for help over anything.) The warden could then touch the gate to teleport to the location. It was important to always take a re-compass with you: a pocket-sized device that would teleport you back home.

Mum hurried into the map room. "I've got to go and sign some paperwork at the Mayor's office," she told Bren and Grace. "Bren, you're in charge of the map." She looked over at Grace, then to Watson. "Watson, I've been thinking," Mum said. "I'd like you to give Grace some extra training. Her co-ordination and focus need a little work."

Grace looked up. "The Mayor shouted and made me jump! That's why I dropped the spyglass the other day." She folded her arms.

Mum walked over and kissed Grace on the head. "They say Great Grandma Griffin was a fidget too," Mum said. "But if you're going to be ready to be a full warden in two years, you need to be more focused."

Grace looked up at the painting of Great Grandma Griffin. The similarities between Grace and her great grandma were remarkable: the long, shiny black hair, high cheekbones and

sharp eyes. In contrast, Mum and Bren had
short blonde hair.

Great Grandma Griffin may have been a
fidget, but she was also brilliant. It was said
that she'd started inventing the map at the
age of thirteen. The same age Grace was now.
Great Grandma Griffin's best friend had been
stuck for three days in a collapsed tunnel in one
of the remote villages. He had died just before
help could reach him. Great Grandma Griffin
had been heartbroken and it had driven her to
invent the map so that people in trouble could
be helped faster.

Mum checked the readings on the map's
digi-screen. "Thank goodness for a quiet week,"
she said to Bren. "I'd better get going. I'll see
you soon." Then she left the room.

Watson flew over to the training area.
"Come along then, Grace," the raven said. "No
time like the present."

Grace rolled up her uniform sleeves. "Bren, why don't you join us?" she suggested. They always used to have fun training together.

"I'm too busy," Bren said, picking a book off the shelf and sitting beside the map.

Grace huffed.

Watson chopped the back of her leg with his wing. Her knees went to jelly. "Hey, I wasn't ready!" Grace cried.

"Combat rule number one: always be ready," Watson said in Mum's voice. Watson had the ability to record speech and play it back whenever he wanted. Grace found it annoying, especially as Watson mostly played back Mum's many warden rules.

They began the training warm-up. This was a routine of stretches and lunges, then a series of arm twists and leg sweeps, all with the aim of keeping flexible and sharp. After the warm-up came combat sparring, where you had to win points by disarming your partner. Mum said you never knew what was going to be on the other side of the gate. It was true that most calls could be solved simply, but wardens should always be ready to defend themselves.

After a while, the front doorbell rang.

"Grace, the door," Bren said, looking up from the manual he was reading and raising his eyebrows.

"I'm busy training and Watson can't go," Grace replied, looking down at Watson. The raven was pinned beneath her grip.

"But I'm in charge of the map," said Bren.

"It's probably just Mum forgetting her key again."

Bren let out a loud sigh and strode into the hallway.

Grace released Watson. Out of the corner of her eye she saw a man at the front door and heard him say, "Spare parts for sale."

"No, thank you, we don't—" Bren started.

"Cogs, fuse boards, micro screws," the man interrupted.

"No, really, we—" Bren tried again.

"Iron web, electro bulbs ..." The man was very persistent.

The cold wintry air from outside blew Grace's way, so she got up and shut the map-room door.

"Right, Watson. Best of five," Grace began, but her attention was suddenly caught by a sapphire-blue light flashing on the map. A call was coming in!

Grace hurried over to the table. The light was in a small village to the far north marked Mudford. Someone there needed help. A strange fizzling started in Grace's stomach. Perhaps this was her chance to prove that the age rule was silly … There was no real reason why Grace couldn't answer a call. She'd had as much training as Bren.

The light changed to red. It was an emergency. Someone needed help right now. Bren was still speaking to the man at the front door and Mum was at the Mayor's. They couldn't blame her for trying to help, surely?

"Don't even think about it!" Watson said, flapping his wings to land on Grace's shoulder. "Bre—" Watson started calling.

Swiftly, Grace clamped her hand around his beak. Her mind was made up. This was her chance to prove herself. She glanced around and saw that Bren had left his re-compass on the arm of his chair. Still holding Watson's beak, Grace dashed over and stuffed the re-compass into her pocket. Then she saw the stun stick she'd just mended beside it and shoved it in her ankle pocket. Watson's muffled protests wouldn't stop her. She dashed back to the map and touched the flashing gate.

3

Celia's Shop

In an instant it was as if Grace's body was being pulled in many directions at once and she was surrounded by bright blue crackling light. She landed with a thud, feeling as if her body had been broken into a thousand parts then jolted back together.

Grace gazed around. She was in a village that looked like something out of a fairy tale, with crooked old buildings, cone rooftops and creeping ivy. Not far away was a tall red box with windows. Great Grandma Griffin had replicated these from old times, Mum had

said. They'd been used for something called
a telephone. People could call the wardens
for help from these red boxes. Mum said you
could teleport anywhere within fifty metres of
the box used to call you. Across the square, a
woman stood in the doorway of a shop called
Celia's Hardware, beckoning Grace in.

Watson dug his claws into Grace's shoulder.

"Ow, I forgot you were with me when I
answered the call," she whispered.

"I can't believe … you just did that," Watson
stammered.

Grace straightened up. She needed to look
as if she did this all the time and wasn't feeling
like she'd just been through a hydro-mill. Grace
approached the woman, who ushered her inside.
"I'm Warden Grace Griffin from Copperport,"
she said. "Someone put in a call for help."

The woman had a golden bun and scared blue eyes. "You're a bit short for a warden," she said.

Grace raised her chin and replied, "I'm fully trained. Was it you that put in the call?" Grace glanced around the shop. Shelves and baskets were full of brushes, mops, jugs, cups, soap and the like. But there didn't seem to be anything amiss.

She hoped that Watson wouldn't say something to give her away, but he still seemed dizzy from the teleport.

The woman stared at Grace. "There's a monster … a monster in the forest," she said. "It raided the village this afternoon. Everyone is terrified."

"A monster?" Grace couldn't help but frown with disbelief.

"That's what I said!" the woman snapped. A bead of sweat ran down her forehead.

"I'm sorry, can I get you a glass of water, Ms ...?" Grace said. Mission rule one was to assess the immediate danger. Rule two: look after the caller.

The woman shook her head. "Call me Celia."

"Oh, of course: Celia's Hardware," Grace replied. "And it's happened just this once?"

"Things have been going missing for weeks," Celia explained. "The villagers have been blaming each other. I saw the monster with my own eyes this afternoon. It disappeared back into the forest. Then I made the call."

Grace whipped out her notebook. Mission rule three: keep notes on the situation.

"And what did this monster look like?" Grace asked.

"Er ... large ... and scary."

"Anything else?" It wasn't much to go on, thought Grace. "Are you sure it wasn't a fox? Maybe a hungry badger?"

The woman's cheeks blushed like shiny red apples. "It was a monster, I tell you!" she insisted.

Grace had to admit that a monster in the forest was a bit more than she'd hoped for. But if she dealt with it, then Mum and Bren would have to agree she was ready to be a full warden – that the age rule was nonsense.

"Are you certain there isn't anything else you can tell me about what you saw?" Grace asked.

Celia thought for a moment. "I think it had red fur."

Grace wrote this in her notebook, then glanced outside, where several villagers had now gathered. She was certain the "monster" would turn out to be a forest animal. Grace decided to interview a few people, then follow the creature's tracks and find the evidence to reassure them all. Then she'd use the re-compass to get back home in time for tea and be praised for her good work.

"Don't worry, Ms … I mean Celia," Grace said. "I'll soon have it sorted."

4

Large and ... Scary

When they were back outside in the square, Watson pecked Grace's ear.

"Ouch! What was that for?" Grace said, rubbing it.

"For being an utter ninny!" Watson replied.

"Do you want me to clamp your beak again?" Grace asked.

"Your mum is going to be furious," Watson went on. "And you've probably got Bren into trouble because he left you alone with the map."

Grace shrugged and looked to the floor. She didn't want Mum to be cross with Bren. They might have drifted apart since he became a proper warden, but he was still her brother. And she hadn't given Bren much choice about leaving her alone with the map. "It'll be fine," Grace told Watson. "We'll find this mystery 'monster'," she said, making quote signs with her fingers, "and then go back. Bren probably won't even have noticed that we're missing yet. Come on, there's a man staring at us in that greengrocers."

Grace strode over. "Hello," she said. "Warden Griffin at your service. Can I ask if you've seen a 'monster' in the area?"

The man had thick white hair, round cheeks and a moustache that almost reached his ears. He nodded and replied, "It's been sneaking in from the forest and stealing things."

"What sort of things, Mr ...?" Grace asked.

"Just call me Bob," he said. "Food, possessions … anything it likes."

"Did you get a good look at it, Bob?"

He only shrugged.

"Can you describe it for me?" Grace went on.

Bob thought for a moment. "It was large … and … scary."

Grace wrote the words in her notebook for the second time. "I see …" she said. "Anything else?"

Bob shook his head.

Grace said goodbye and moved along to the next shop, called Knit 'n' Needle. It had rolls of colourful wool in the window. She moved to grasp the door handle, but someone on the other side whipped it open as if they'd been waiting for her.

"Oh!" Grace said, startled. She looked down at a small chubby man wearing a rainbow-stripe knitted jumper.

"Are you the warden?" he asked.

Grace nodded. "Can you tell me anything about the 'monster' that's been raiding Mudford, Mr ...?"

"Call me Fred," the small man said.

Grace thought everyone was very friendly in this village, since they'd introduced themselves by their first names. "What can you tell me, Fred?" Grace asked.

"Well, it was very large—"

"—and scary," Watson interrupted, replaying what Celia had said.

Grace held back a snigger.

"How did you know?" Fred asked.

"Instinct," said Grace. "Now, can you tell me anything else about it at all?"

Fred shook his head.

"Did you at least notice where it entered the forest? You see, I could follow its tracks and lay a trap."

Grace felt a tap on her arm. She turned around and saw a young golden-haired woman in an apron. "Hello. I'm Loralie, the village smithy. The monster disappeared not far from my place over there. I'll show you."

Loralie led them to the forest edge. "That's where it went back in," she said. "Right there. I'll leave you to it." Then she hurried away.

Grace looked into the silent gloom of the forest.

"There's only one thing for it, Watson," she said.

"I force you to the ground, take the re-compass from your pocket and teleport us back home?" Watson suggested. "Then apologise to your mum for not keeping you under control?"

Grace clamped his beak again. "We're going to check out the forest. Come on."

5

Into the Forest

The sun hung low in the western sky. Hazy clouds made it look more like the moon. Grace shivered. It was colder in the north than back in Copperport and a coating of frost spread across the forest.

Grace bent down to examine the ground. "There has been some movement here. Look, Watson – the leaves have been crushed in regular patterns." Grace thought the prints looked bigger than those a fox would make, but it was hard to tell. "And see how the twigs are snapped on the ground here and here?" She pointed.

"Yes, I can see," said Watson.

"Come on."

Grace trudged further into the trees, Watson on her shoulder.

The air had an icy bite and everything smelled of damp earth and fungi. Grace's breath puffed out in chugs of white.

Watson flew to a branch in front of her and spread his wings. "We shouldn't go too far," he said. "I mean, what if the villagers are right and there is a monster?"

"Watson, they've just worked themselves up into a frenzy," Grace told him. "There will be a perfectly rational explanation. We can't give up now." She tapped her shoulder so Watson would fly back to her, and they continued into the trees.

After a short while, something caught Grace's eye. "Look! There's some fur down here." She pulled it off a low twig. "It's even red like a fox's. See, I told you! Come on, its den is probably not far away."

"A fox that steals vegetables and wool?" Watson said.

"Perhaps it's a highly intelligent fox," Grace replied. "Maybe something like you."

"A robot?"

"It's not only Copperport that's advanced, you know. Look, more tracks!"

A twig snapped a short distance away.

"What was that?" said Watson.

Grace looked around, her eyes wide. "Just a small creature. Probably a rabbit."

"Maybe we should turn back," said Watson.

"Nonsense. We can't give up now."

"All right, little miss smarty pants, how about this? If it *is* a fox, then why is there fur at the height of our heads?"

Grace paused to look at some fur caught on a high branch. "Perhaps it's very good at jumping?" she said with a nervous laugh, because Watson was right. It *was* strange.

Somewhere not far away, something squawked loudly.

"Agh!" Grace cried, jumping. Watson's claws clutched her shoulder tightly. Then they both realised it was only a bird.

They looked at each other and laughed.

"We're just being silly because we're alone in a gloomy, cold forest and it feels scary," Grace decided. "But really there's nothing to be—"

A growl rumbled through the trees, cutting Grace off. Nearby leaves quivered.

Every muscle in Grace's body became stiff. Her eyes stretched as wide as saucers. "That wasn't a fox," she whispered.

6

The Den

"Look, it's a den!" Grace said in a hushed voice as she pointed between the trees at a large huddle of branches, twigs and moss.

She took a breath. She had rope, a stun stick and her determination to prove herself – she could do this.

The growling noise was coming from inside the den, but as Grace and Watson neared, they could hear that the sound was repeating in a regular pattern.

"I think it's asleep, Watson!" Grace said. "Come on, we'll tie it up before it wakes. I've got the rope and the stun stick, just in case."

They sneaked around the outside of the domed den. Grace took several long breaths, then carefully peered into the opening. It was dark, but she could make out the outline of a large red furry mound. "Be brave," she whispered.

"I will," said Watson.

Grace didn't have the heart to say she was talking to herself.

"I'll put the rope around its neck, tie it to one of the trees outside and go back to tell the villagers. Then ..." Grace trailed off as she realised she had no idea what to do next. She wanted to say, "Then we'll go back and ask Mum and Bren for help", but she couldn't. How could she prove herself if she gave in and asked for help? Perhaps the creature would be friendly and she could simply lead it to a safe place away from the village? It looked a bit like a bear, although it was hard to see in the dark.

Grace took a small step inside the den, so that her body was half in and half out.

Suddenly, the soft growling snore stopped.

Grace froze. The hairs on her arms prickled.

Slowly, the animal's head rose from the ground. Its eyes opened and stared right at Grace – two blood-red circles that shone like fierce rubies. It wasn't a bear.

"Back away," whispered Watson.

But Grace felt as if her boots were stuck to the ground. Her heart thumped in her ribcage. The creature opened its mouth and its teeth shone in the dark like kitchen knives.

"Grace, run!" Watson screeched.

The monster let out a roar that made Grace's chest rumble.

She turned on her heels and scrambled away. Her feet slipped from beneath her and she fell flat on her face. She yelped in terror. Watson tumbled to the ground, wings sprawled. Hot breath snapped at Grace's ankles as she ...

Wait.

Hot breath wasn't snapping at her ankles.

In fact, everything had gone quiet.

In a daze from her panicked thoughts, Grace hurriedly got to her feet. She scooped Watson from the leaves as she moved and put him on her shoulder. Grace turned around to face the den. The growling snore had returned. How could the creature go back to sleep so quickly?

Grace looked at Watson and shrugged, feeling confused.

Slowly, she stepped back to the entrance and peered in once more. The monster was asleep. She took half a step inside. Just as before, its head rose, its red eyes opened. It roared. Grace reared back, but this time she kept facing the creature. As she moved, the monster's head flopped back down and the snoring growl resumed.

Grace looked at Watson and as she did she noticed a thin beam of red light across the cave entrance. "It's some sort of trigger," she whispered. She waved her hand where the laser shone. Again, the creature awoke and roared but didn't attack. Grace let her hand fall and it went back to sleep.

"Can you hear that strange ticking?" she asked Watson, tilting her head to listen. Grace was certain she could hear something mechanical.

"It's not real!" they both said, the realisation hitting Grace and Watson at the same time.

"It must be some kind of joke," said Grace, her brain suddenly full of questions. "Come on, let's take a closer look." She moved to step forwards and the creature awoke once more. Just as she was about to place her foot down, Grace had a thought. If there was one trigger, there could be more. She froze and looked about, spotting something on the floor. Grace carefully stepped back, then crouched to take a look. Cautiously, she scuffed back the dirt on the floor to reveal a hidden button.

Watson tilted his large feathered head, his bead-like eyes blinking. "What's that for?" he asked.

Grace turned her head to look up. Something glinted in the dim light of the den and Grace realised that a large cage swung above them.

"Watson, it's a trap!" Grace said. "If we'd taken a full step onto that button, the cage would have come down and we'd be stuck in it right now."

"But who would do a thing like that?"

"I'm as confused as you." This mission wasn't turning out as Grace had hoped. "We could go back and ask the villagers," she said. "But they'll probably be as puzzled as us, and it'll be dark soon, so we won't have time to look further in the forest." She sighed. "We have to go home."

Watson flapped. *"Finally* you understand."

"Maybe we can hurry back to the village, tell them it's nothing to worry about, then make it home before Mum gets back. Then we can all come back together and find out who's behind it." Grace put her hand in her pocket to get the re-compass. But it was empty. She tried another pocket. It wasn't there either.

Her heart jolted. "Watson. Have you got the re-compass?" Grace asked.

Watson spread his wings. "And I suppose I'm keeping it in my big pockets?" he said in a sarcastic tone.

"Funny." Grace tutted, but panic was tightening her throat. "Maybe you put it somewhere?"

Watson ruffled his feathers. "You've lost the re-compass, haven't you?"

"No!" Grace snapped. "Well ... maybe. It must've fallen out in the forest. How about we retrace our steps and search on the way?"

"I don't see that we have much choice," Watson said. "Come on."

7

Teleporting: Rule One

Grace and Watson had spent an hour searching the undergrowth and now it was sunset and Grace was shivering with cold. They decided their only choice was to go back to the village.

"Perhaps Mum and Bren will come looking for us anyway?" said Grace.

"When you broke the first teleporting rule?" Watson said.

Grace knew that Watson was right. The realisation was like an iron ball landing in her stomach. "Teleporting rule one: leave a note of your destination," Grace said wearily. In her rush to prove herself she'd completely forgotten to do it. "But I took the re-compass. It's not my fault it disappeared into thin air."

"You mean you dropped it ..." Watson said. He flew up to a branch above and looked down at Grace. "So, we're stuck here. Nice work, Warden."

Grace frowned. "I know! Maybe the re-compass fell out of my pocket when we teleported. We did get quite a jolt. It could be in the village square! If we hurry, we might still get back without Mum finding out what I've done!"

"Grace, that's the most sensible thing you've said all day."

Grace let out a long breath. "I'm not looking forward to telling Mum I've lost the re-compass," she said, "so let's just hope it's there."

When they arrived back in Mudford, the shops around the square looked shut. They searched the ground for the re-compass, but there was nothing there.

"Come on, there's still a light on in Celia's Hardware," said Grace. "Maybe I dropped it in the shop."

They hurried across the square. "I can't see Celia in the shop," Watson said.

Grace tried the handle. It was open. "Hello?" she called. All was quiet.

"We can't go in if there's no one here," said Watson.

"We're just going in to look for the re-compass," Grace said. "If we find it, we'll leave a note about the fake monster and get out of here."

They searched carefully around the floor of the shop but soon had to admit that the re-compass wasn't there.

"Maybe Celia found it and put it behind the counter for us," Grace said, and began rooting around. "I can't see it, but ..." She paused. There was a spyglass on the counter. "Look, Watson! It's just like Mayor Pick's, the one he gave to Bren. It has the Mayor's crest and the same gold wave pattern." Grace picked it up. "How curious."

The floorboards creaked and Grace turned to see Celia in the doorway, a shocked look on her round face. "You're back," Celia said. "Thank goodness you're all right."

"Yes, we are," Grace replied.

"What are you doing?" Celia said suddenly, rushing over to grab the spyglass.

Grace frowned. "I'm sorry. I was just looking for a small compass. It looks a bit like a disc. I may have dropped it when I arrived. Did you find it?"

Celia shook her head. "I'm afraid I don't know what you're talking about."

Grace slumped and felt Watson's soft wing brush her neck to comfort her. She looked at him, wrinkled her nose and sighed. This day was turning out nothing like she'd hoped.

Celia clutched the spyglass like a precious jewel.

"Do you know Mayor Pick?" asked Grace.

Celia's cheeks flushed red as she replied, "Not personally."

"It's just that I thought perhaps with you having one of his spyglasses—"

"It was awarded to me ... for best village flower display this summer," Celia explained.

Grace frowned and looked to the door. Outside, it was now almost dark. She had a growing feeling of panic, until she realised something. "Wait, Watson, we can go to the red box and put in a call for help! Mum will know it's us."

"Ah, not good news on that front, I'm afraid," said Celia. "There's a problem with the red box."

"A problem?" Grace said, wondering if things could get any worse.

"Don't think badly of me," Celia went on, "but when you went into the forest, I wasn't sure you were very …"

"Very what?" Grace asked, with a sinking feeling of not being trusted.

"… capable," Celia finished. "So I went to put in another call, but I found that the call box had been damaged."

"Damaged?"

"Wires all over the place. Local troublemakers probably."

Grace looked out at the town square. She would bet that whoever the troublemakers were, they were also behind the fake monster. But what were they trying to do?

Grace realised that in her panic about getting home, she'd forgotten to tell Celia what they'd found.

"The monster is fake, by the way," Grace said. "We did succeed in finding it, but it's mechanical. There's even a trap."

"Really?" said Celia, leaning in. "It isn't real?"

Grace shook her head. "Someone has been messing with you. Perhaps it's the same person that damaged the red box?"

"Are you sure it isn't real?" asked Celia.

"The monster is all lights, sound effects and wires."

"How curious," said Celia. "I can't imagine why anyone would do such a thing."

Grace suddenly felt a pull to her chest and a horrible empty feeling deep inside. She wanted to be with Mum and Bren. She didn't want to be stuck hundreds of miles from home. "What are we going to do, Watson?" Grace said, turning to her faithful family friend. "How are we going to get home?"

"I know," said Celia. "Why don't you stay here tonight and we can search again for your compass thing in the morning?"

Grace looked at Watson, knowing that they didn't have much of a choice.

"That's settled then," said Celia. "I have a spare room and it's all ready."

Grace looked out of the shop window into the deep shadows of the forest. Who or what was behind this?

8

Midnight Footsteps

Watson perched on the end of the bed snoring, while Grace stared at the ceiling trying to work everything out. Nothing made sense. She'd been awake for hours thinking about the day's events.

Just then, a door clicked and Grace heard footsteps in the hallway. Grace listened as the sound faded, then she heard muffled voices coming from the shop below.

Grace swung her feet out of bed. "Watson!" she whispered urgently. "Wake up."

"It's the middle of the night," he groaned.

"You're a robot bird. You don't actually need to sleep. Celia's talking to someone and I want to know who. Come on, we're going to find out."

Grace turned the door handle silently and crept along the hall. She peered around the corner of the stairway.

Watson flew to join her. "There are definitely two voices," he said. "There must be someone down there with Celia."

"Exactly," Grace said. "We need to get closer."

"Grace!" Watson whispered.

But Watson had no choice, as Grace was already moving down the stairs towards the voices.

A red curtain separated the stairs from the shop.

"It's all working out," they heard Celia say. "I have the girl under control."

"Are you quite sure?" said a different voice.

"Absolutely," Celia replied.

"And the monster?"

"Ah. A slight hitch," Celia said. "The girl's brave, and smarter than you thought. She saw the trap trigger button and figured it out."

"Celia, the entire plan could be in jeopardy!"

"She doesn't suspect it's us. I convinced her it was local troublemakers, and now she's upstairs, sound asleep."

Grace's eyes widened with shock at the unfolding conversation. She had to cross her arms to contain her urge to rush out and confront Celia. Grace needed to hear more first.

"How are things at your end?" Celia asked.

"It's all going to plan," the unknown voice said. "The boy has no idea that he was being watched through the spyglass."

Grace frowned to herself. Who was being watched? And she was sure she recognised the other voice – was it one of the other villagers she'd met? Carefully, Grace pulled the curtain back a bit to take a peek. She was surprised to see Celia sitting alone, talking to her spyglass.

"How long do I have to keep her here, Clem?" Celia asked.

Clem? Grace racked her brain. Why was the name familiar? Then she realised. It must be Mayor Clemence Pick! It was his voice she'd recognised. Could the boy he was talking about

be Bren? And why did Celia and Mayor Pick
want to keep Grace here?

"We stick to the plan," Mayor Pick said.
"The Lawmakers of Copperport think that Grace
Griffin has been captured by the monster.

I have told them that I have witnesses from the village who say blood was found at the scene. Grace Griffin is presumed dead. They'll keep Ann Griffin locked away for certain. The map is Ann's responsibility and everyone will believe that it was her neglect that led to the girl's death."

Grace let go of the curtain and clamped her hand over her mouth to stop a gasp from escaping. Her heart dropped to the bottom of her chest. Poor Mum! And what did this mean for Grace herself?

"Keep making excuses in the morning," Mayor Pick continued. "My contact will arrive in Mudford before noon to take the girl on the next boat to the frozen north. She's been sold to the iron mines."

Grace couldn't breathe. She looked at Watson, her eyes wide.

"And the robot bird?" asked Celia.

"Catch it and get Loralie to melt it to nothing," Mayor Pick instructed. "We'll speak again tomorrow."

Watson gulped and pointed a wing upstairs. "We can get out of the bedroom window," he whispered.

Grace nodded, but the staircase seemed to be swimming in front of her eyes. She felt dizzy and sick. Mum thought she was dead. She had been sold across the far sea to the iron mines. Why was the Mayor doing all this?

"Come on!" Watson whispered.

Grace took a step up the staircase but stumbled.

"What was that?" said Celia suddenly.

Grace froze, as if panic had gripped her in a vice. The curtain was whipped back and, before Grace could move, Celia grabbed her. Grace tried to react, to use some of her training, but her whole body felt numb with the shock of it all. Watson squawked and took flight. Celia reached her other hand out for him, but he was too fast and flew upstairs.

"Stupid bird," Celia said. "I'll get you later."

Grace tried to fight, but it was as if her arms and legs were filled with sand.

Celia twisted Grace's arms behind her back and dragged her towards the back of the shop. "Why couldn't you have been caught in the trap like you were meant to?" Celia said.

Something inside Grace kicked back into life. She had to get out of here. She ducked and twisted away, then bolted for the door. She reached the handle, but Celia grabbed Grace and pulled her to the ground.

"You're not going anywhere," Celia said, her voice hard and cruel.

Celia grabbed a rope from a basket and tied Grace's hands behind her. She then flipped open a panel in the floor, revealing stairs that led down to a cellar. Celia hauled Grace to her feet, then pushed her into the hole.

Grace lurched down the steps, fighting to keep her balance. "Watson will find the re-compass and come back for me," she told Celia. "You won't get away with this."

Celia laughed. "We already have." She fiddled with her silk neck scarf.

Grace looked up from the cellar and caught a flash of gold around Celia's neck: a chain and ... "*You* took the re-compass!" said Grace. It was like another punch to the chest.

"It was all too easy while you were busy scribbling notes in that book of yours earlier," Celia sneered.

Then the cellar door shut, plunging Grace into darkness.

9

The Mayor's Plan

Grace wriggled and writhed until she finally broke free of the rope. She bashed at the cellar door, but it was bolted shut and nothing would shift it. Eventually, Grace curled up at the bottom of the stairs and sobbed with frustration. She fell into a restless sleep filled with nightmares about her mum imprisoned many miles away in Copperport believing Grace was dead.

The sound of metal scraping woke Grace. She grabbed something that felt like a can of paint and hurried up the stairs, ready to strike.

Last night she hadn't had the strength or the quick thinking, but now she felt ready to act. Grace swung the can behind her and thrust it forwards with all her might as the door lifted upwards.

Watson squawked in alarm and flew back. "That's a fine way to greet your rescuer!" he said.

"Watson!" Grace squeaked, hurrying out. She grabbed the raven and hugged him tight. "How did you get away? Where's Celia?"

"I escaped up the chimney – it was a bit of a squeeze, but I made it and stayed on the roof for the night. At first light, I tapped on Celia's window. She chased me into the forest, but I led her deep into it, then lost her and doubled back. I flew back down the chimney and here we are."

Grace had never been so happy to see someone. "Great work, Watson."

Watson tilted his head. "Are you all right?" he asked.

Her eyes were sore, but Grace nodded. "I have to be. Celia will soon realise what you've done and be back. We need to move fast."

"When I was flying, there wasn't any sign of another town," Watson said. "But if we follow the lane we're bound to find somewhere if we keep going. Come on."

Grace shook her head. No matter how much she wanted to run, she couldn't help but think that there was a better way. "Watson," Grace began, "last night when Mayor Pick was talking to Celia, he said that Bren had no idea he was being watched. The spyglass the Mayor gave to Bren is all part of his plan. The Mayor used it to spy on us." She heaved in a long breath. "But why?" Grace paused to think, then stared at Watson. "What if we use Celia's spyglass now to spy on the Mayor to find out?"

"I'll keep watch from the window, you get the spyglass," Watson said keenly.

Grace took the spyglass from its stand beneath the counter and extended the body. She held it up to her eye, pointed it towards the shop window ... and let out a long huff. All she could see were the trees beyond the village square. "There has to be something more to this," Grace said.

She examined the case: the gold wave patterns decorated the main body and Mayor Pick's family crest was at the larger end. There were no obvious buttons. "Maybe it has something to do with the pattern," Grace muttered, noticing how it was raised rather than engraved in the rosewood. "Perhaps ..."

She clasped her hand around the spyglass and twisted hard. The wave pattern shifted, something clicked into place and the pattern shone amber. Grace's heart jumped. "It's working!" she called to Watson. She had to admit she was impressed by the clever way the mechanism was hidden. "The pattern on the body moves and connects something."

Grace put it to her eye again. Now she could see Mayor Pick in his Copperport office. He was talking to one of his assistants. "I can see Mayor Pick, but I can't hear him," Grace called to Watson.

"Try twisting it again," Watson suggested.

After another small turn, the wave pattern turned green and the Mayor's voice came from the spyglass. Grace glanced at Watson and put her finger to her lips. If they could hear *him*, Mayor Pick might be able to hear *them*.

"... reduced to a constant stream of paperwork," the Mayor said. "The Picks were the most important family in Copperport once, you know. We were admired by everyone until the Griffins came along and took the spotlight. It's time to reclaim full control in Copperport and regain our position as the most powerful family in all of Moreland."

"And you're sure you can get the Griffin map?" the Mayor's assistant asked.

"I already have it," Mayor Pick replied. "It's deactivated in the back room." He waved a hand towards a door behind him. "The Lawmakers will soon officially assign the map to me for good – once Ann Griffin is found guilty of misuse of the map and of neglect leading to the death of her daughter. After all, I am the natural choice as Mayor. The Picks will be the most powerful family in Moreland once more."

"What about the Griffin boy?" the assistant said.

"He'll be thinking it's his fault for leaving the girl alone with the map. Ann Griffin will be locked away and I will assign him to an orphanage where he can be cared for. One far away!" The Mayor laughed. "How simple it was to lure the Griffin girl into our little trap! So young and eager and easily fooled. All we needed was a distraction so that she was alone with the map."

It hit Grace like a bolt to her chest – the assistant was the salesman who had come to the front door of Griffin House the day before. In her moment of fury, she squeezed the spyglass and the family crest gave way, pressing like a button. The spyglass started flashing red.

The Mayor looked up suddenly.

Grace held her breath.

"There's a call coming in from Celia," said the Mayor.

Panic froze Grace's blood. Could Mayor Pick see her? No, he'd have to be looking into the lens. But he was now walking straight towards her! Quickly, Grace pressed the crest button, faced the spyglass away from her and twisted the pattern, which now shone green again.

She put it on the counter facing the wall and hurried over to Watson. "Did you hear that?" Grace said. "Not only was the Mayor going to send me overseas, he was going to send Bren away too. The Mayor knew how much I wanted to be a warden and he made sure I was alone with the map when Celia made her call!"

"Despicable," said Watson.

Grace nodded. "But at least we know where the map is now." A plan was forming in her mind. "Is there any sign of Celia?" she asked Watson.

"No, but she won't be long."

"Keep watching," Grace said. "I know what to do. The spyglasses are linked. Mayor Pick's connects to Celia's and Bren's, and we know that Celia's connects to Mayor Pick's, so perhaps ..."

"Perhaps what?" Watson asked.

"Maybe Celia's spyglass can connect to Bren's too, like a triangle?"

Watson opened his wings and ruffled them excitedly. "Grace, I think you could be right!"

"We can contact Bren and tell him what's going on," Grace said. "He can help us get home!"

Grace hurried back to the spyglass and slowly put it to her eye. She crossed her fingers, hoping that the last turn had disconnected the Mayor and …

Her heart leapt.

She could see Bren.

10

Wing Chop

"Bren!" Grace shouted as she watched Bren pacing the map room back at Griffin House. "Watson, I can see home!"

"Grace, Celia's coming out of the forest," Watson said. "Hurry!"

Grace remembered she needed to press the crest. It flashed red. She hoped it was doing the same at Bren's end.

The flashing light must have caught Bren's eye, as he looked straight over and frowned.

"Bren, it's me!" Grace yelled.

He shook his head as if he was imagining it. "Grace?"

"On the mantelpiece," Grace said. "I'm in the spyglass!" She glanced up at Watson. "How long do we have?"

"Celia's stopped to talk to Fred, but you must hurry," Watson urged.

Grace put her eye back to the spyglass. "Bren, pick it up," she told her brother. "Hold the casing hard and twist the pattern until it clicks so you can see me, and if you see the Mayor, turn it again!"

Bren did as she said and put the spyglass to his eye. Grace held hers away a little so Bren could see her in full. "What in Copperport?!" Bren yelped. "Grace, you're alive!" He clasped a hand to his mouth and his eyes pooled with tears.

"I'm fine, but we don't have much time," Grace said. "The spyglass is a two-way viewer so we can communicate. Hold it away a bit so I can see you properly." Grace quickly explained what had happened and everything she knew so far.

Bren's mouth dropped wide. "What do we do?" he asked.

"I have a plan." Grace looked over to Watson. "You heard everything that the Mayor said just now and to Celia last night, didn't you?"

"Yes," Watson said. "Loud and clear."

"Good. Then we'll be able to replay it to the Lawmakers – it's proof that Mayor Pick plotted all of this so that he would be able to take control of the map."

Watson nodded.

"But first I need you to do something really important, Bren," Grace said, looking into the spyglass again. "I want you to break into Mayor Pick's house and activate the map so that we can return home."

"How will I know where to find it?" Bren asked.

"The Mayor has the map in the room behind his office," Grace said. "I'll let you know when the coast is clear by spying from here. Hurry there now and wait outside."

"Celia's stopped talking," Watson called. "She's on her way back!"

"I've got to go," Grace told her brother. "Run, and don't forget to take the spyglass."

Grace pressed the crest to make the lights go out and put the spyglass back to a neutral setting. She swiftly ducked behind the counter of the shop and Watson flew to land beside her.

"We need to get rid of Celia so that we can get Bren to the map. Any ideas?" Watson whispered.

"As a matter of fact, yes," Grace replied. "You know that wing chop that you do in training? The one that always gets me?"

Watson nodded.

"Hide behind that basket and be ready when I give the signal."

The bell above the door clanged.

Footsteps neared. Just before Celia reached the counter, Grace leapt from behind it.

Celia gasped. "How did you get out?" she demanded.

"I know all about your plan and what Mayor Pick is up to," Grace said, scowling.

Celia laughed. It sounded cruel and harsh. "And what are you going to do about it, little girl? You're all alone, miles from home, with Mummy in prison thinking you're dead!"

In a flash, Grace whipped the cellar door open. "Now!" she shouted at Watson.

Watson flew to Celia and chopped the back of her knees with his wing. Celia yelped and lurched forwards. As she fell, Grace reached out and grabbed the re-compass from her neck, then pushed her into the cellar. Celia sprawled halfway down the stairs, but before she could turn to escape, Grace slammed the door and pulled the bolt across.

"Excellent work!" said Watson.

Grace smiled and rushed to grab the spyglass. She twisted it to look at the Mayor's office. The Mayor wasn't there. She twisted it twice more to find Bren. For a while, all Grace could see was the ground rushing past, then Bren must have lifted up the spyglass, as she saw he was standing in front of the Mayor's house, sweating from the run.

"Grace, are you there?" Bren asked.

"Bren," Grace replied. "The Mayor's not in his office. The coast is clear, but you'll need to be careful because he might still be in the house somewhere." Grace paused, jolted by a sudden realisation. "I didn't think about how you're going to get in ..."

"Warden training," said Bren. He held up a brass key with a pronged electrical tip. "It's Great Grandma Griffin's every-key. We should only break in to a building if absolutely necessary and this is one of those times."

Grace watched as Bren quietly unlocked the door and crept into the hallway. "Be careful," she whispered. "His assistants might be lurking."

Bren waited a moment, listening intently, then continued along the hallway. "There's no one about," he said. "I'm going straight to the Mayor's office."

But no sooner had Bren said that than footsteps sounded above. Bren froze. "Someone's coming," he whispered. Bren ducked behind the stairs and opened a small door underneath. He crept inside and shut it. Everything went black. "I'm in a broom cupboard," he whispered.

Grace watched, holding her breath, scared to make a sound. Footsteps echoed above as someone walked down the stairs, then along the hallway.

The footsteps stopped and someone started speaking. "Potts, the Mayor has a list of chores. He wants a new sign made urgently, to read: Mayor Pick, Law Enforcer of Moreland and Warden of the Pick Map. Take it to the sign writer's straight away. He wants it back before the banquet this evening. It's to be a celebration of a new era for Moreland with the Picks in charge."

Grace wanted to cry out in rage. More footsteps sounded then faded.

"I think it's safe now," Bren whispered after a moment. He crept back out and hurried up the stairs, then along the hall towards the Mayor's office. He reached for the door handle.

"What do you think you're doing?"

Bren spun around at the voice.

"Er … I'm returning this," Bren said. He held up the spyglass and Grace caught a view of one of the Mayor's assistants narrowing her eyes. "You see, it was a gift and I don't deserve it, not any more," Bren went on. "Not after we failed as wardens and my sister got killed because we left her alone with the map. Mayor Pick sent a note saying I should put it back in his office. Another assistant told me to go straight up."

The assistant thought for a moment, then said, "Wait there. I'll get rid of these tablecloths and escort you."

As soon as she went down the stairs, Bren bolted into the office.

"It's in the room at the back – hurry!" Grace urged.

Bren rushed over and opened the door. "There it is," he said. "But I need to activate it!" He hurried to the digi-screen and began typing. The gates on the map flashed to life.

In an instant, Watson flew to Grace's shoulder and Grace pressed the button on the re-compass.

11

The Truth

Grace's body was pulled in a thousand directions once more as she was lost in bright blue crackling light. She landed with a thud beside the map. Bren rushed to her before Grace could even open her mouth to speak, squeezing her tight. "Thank goodness you're all right!" he said.

"Who's there? What's all that noise?!"

It was the Mayor's voice. Bren looked to the door. "Mayor Pick must have come back. He's in his office! Quick, Grace, you go out of the window and I'll distract him." Bren pulled it open. "Go to the Lawmakers and find Mum."

The door opened and the round, red face of the Mayor was there. "What are you doing?" Mayor Pick demanded, glancing over at Grace. His face dropped as he recognised her. In a moment he was dashing forwards.

"Go!" Bren called as he jumped between the Mayor and Grace.

Grace leapt onto the roof below before she could hear any more. She ran across the rooftop and scurried down the drainpipe, hurrying towards the Copperport Lawmakers building with Watson flying above.

She burst through the door. Two Lawmakers were behind the desk.

"Wait there, young lady!" one said. "You can't just charge in here like that!"

Grace put her hands on her knees and gasped for breath. "My ... mum," Grace panted. "Ann ... Griffin."

"Yes, we have her here. She allowed a minor into the map and the girl died. Hold on ... you're Grace Griffin, the girl that was killed!"

Grace gestured to herself. "As you can see, I'm not dead. It was the Mayor. He made up this story about me dying because he wants the power of the map for himself!"

The Lawmakers looked at Grace and frowned. Then they laughed. "How ridiculous. As if the Mayor of Copperport would do that. Is this some kind of game you've come up with? Because your family is already in a lot of trouble."

Mayor Pick burst through the door. "It's all lies!" he boomed. "Whatever she says, don't believe it."

"You don't have to believe me," Grace said. "But you can't deny the words from the Mayor's own mouth!" Grace nodded to Watson, who flew to land on the desk. He opened his beak wide and began replaying what he'd recorded the Mayor saying through the spyglass back in Mudford.

When Watson had finished, shocked silence filled the room. The Lawmakers looked between each other in disbelief.

Mayor Pick's jaw dropped open.

"Mayor Pick, can you give us any explanation for what we've just heard?" said one Lawmaker.

"I ... I ... this is outrageous!" the Mayor screamed.

"Evidence suggests that you plotted to get Grace Griffin stuck in the map. You wanted her family to believe she was dead. Do you have anything to say?" the other Lawmaker asked.

Mayor Pick was bright red with both fury and the truth of what he had done.

Grace put her hands on her hips. "Watson," she said, "perhaps you could replay the part where Mayor Pick was planning to send me off to the iron mines for ever?"

"But I didn't *actually* harm you!" the Mayor protested. "I was only going to ship you off to the iron mines and send the boy to an orphanage. That map should be mine! I should be the one controlling the power in this country."

"The map wasn't made for those in charge to feel powerful," Grace said firmly. "It was made to help people in need."

The Lawmakers looked at each other and nodded. Then one of them took Mayor Pick by the arm and declared, "Clemence Pick, I'm arresting you for plotting to corrupt justice in Copperport, for concealing the truth and for your unlawful attempt to seize power."

"Lawmaker Higgs," the other Lawmaker said, "take Mr Pick to a cell and release Ann Griffin immediately."

"I'm the Mayor of Copperport!" the Mayor yelled. "You can't do this!"

Lawmaker Higgs took Clemence Pick's mayor badge. "Not any more. Lawmakers consider the misuse of power a very serious offence. You won't be allowed out for a long time."

Bren appeared in the doorway. "Is everything all right?" he asked, looking at Grace, who nodded and smiled widely. They watched Mayor Pick being dragged away.

Bren pulled Grace into another hug. "Great work, Warden," he said.

12

Wardens

Ann Griffin came out of the prison cell concerned and confused. She looked as if she hadn't slept in a while. Then she saw Grace and gasped, putting her shaking hand to her mouth. Grace ran to her mum and hugged her tightly.

Bren explained everything.

Then Grace added, "The Lawmakers have worked out that the whole village of Mudford must have been in on the Mayor's plan to capture me and ship me off to the iron mines. Most of the people in Mudford are related to the Mayor, which is probably why they all only used their first names with me. Apparently, his family is from there. They must have made the fake monster and even planted the fur on the trees and created the footprints. The villagers were certain I'd be caught in their trap in the den. The Lawmakers are on their way to arrest them too."

Mum took Grace's hand. "I'm so sorry I underestimated you, Grace," she said. "Your observations and quick thinking saved the day. You've done brilliantly." She looked over at Watson. "And you too!" Mum told the raven.

"And I'm sorry for going behind your back into the map and putting everyone at risk," said Grace.

Mum smiled. "You know, Grandma Griffin invented that map because she wanted to use her skills to help people. She made it part of the family tradition because she knew that together the Griffins are a strong team. And you are an important part of the team, Grace."

Bren looked across and said, "Hey, Grace. Maybe we could train together again? I miss it. I only stopped because I knew you were getting so good that you kept beating me!"

Grace grinned and the warm feeling of happiness filled her.

The family left the Lawmakers and collected the Griffin map on the way home.

Once they'd arrived back at Griffin House, they set the map back up on the table.

Not long after, a gate on the map flashed red. The three of them stared at it and Watson flew over to look.

"It's Greenwell Beyond the Marshes," said Bren.

Mum took a closer look at the map. "They've probably been flooded and need some help," she said. "Or maybe the bogwamps have invaded again."

"You'd better hurry, Mum," said Grace.

Ann Griffin reached out her hand for Bren. "Come on, we'd better go together," she told him. "It might get sticky." She turned to Watson. "Can you keep an eye out back here?"

Grace's heart sank a little. Of course Mum would leave Watson in charge rather than her after what she'd done.

Watson saluted with his wing. "I may look like a raven, but I'm a Griffin through and through. Griffin HQ is safely under my wing."

"I knew I could rely on you," Mum said, and turned to Grace. "And I know I can rely on *you* too." Mum took Grace's hand and asked, "Are you ready for another mission?"

"Me?" Grace said. "But I still have two years to wait before I can become a warden."

Her mum nodded. "Some rules are made to be broken."

Grace smiled widely. She wrote the words *Gone to Greenwell* on the pad of paper beside the map.

Bren took the re-compass and zipped it in his pocket.

"Activate the gate, Warden Griffin," said Mum, looking at Grace.

Grace reached towards the gate.

With a whirl and a flash of blue, the three of them disappeared into the map.

Together.

Our books are tested
for children and young people by
children and young people.

Thanks to everyone who consulted on
a manuscript for their time and effort in
helping us to make our books better
for our readers.